The Leaf that Wouldn't Leave

Written by Trish Trinco
Illustrated by Bryan Langdo

TRISTAN Publishing
Minneapolis

Library of Congress Cataloging-in-Publication Data

Trinco, Trish, 1955-
  The leaf that wouldn't leave / by Trish Trinco ; illustrated by Bryan Langdo.
     p. cm.
  Summary: Luigi, a birch leaf, finally accepts the advice of nearby Evelyn Evergreen
and lets go of the tree that has always been his home to fly into the autumn sky.
  ISBN 978-0-931674-90-7 (alk. paper)
  [1. Stories in rhyme. 2. Leaves--Fiction. 3. Change--Fiction. 4. Autumn--Fiction.]
  I. Langdo, Bryan, ill. II. Title. III. Title: The leaf that would not leave.
  PZ8.3.T6955Lec 2008
  [E]--dc22

                                                                2008026877

TRISTAN Publishing, Inc.
2355 Louisiana Avenue North
Golden Valley, MN 55427

Printed in China
First Printing

Please visit www.tristanpublishing.com

Dedicated to the brave little leaf
who flew inside my car one fun fall day
and took me on the ride of my life!

Trish Trinco

It's been a long time, but I'll try to remember
What happened one day, near the end of September.

That's what we call the beginning of autumn,
When trees start to change, from the top to the bottom.

Their leaves become yellow, and some will turn red,
While others are bright as an orange instead.

The leaves in the trees all look forward to fall;
They say it's the very best season of all.

They love to change colors and join in the fun
And fly off the branches – well, all except one.

There's one leaf who didn't like change in the weather.
In fact, he just didn't like change altogether.

This shy little leaf lived on top of a birch,
Where bees like to buzz, and the birds like to perch.

A little girl planted this tree in the spring,
In the back of her yard, standing next to her swing.

This leaf – named Luigi – would never branch out,
And he is the one that this story's about.

He'd never admit it, but he's in a rut.
He's the very last leaf on his tree, but so what?

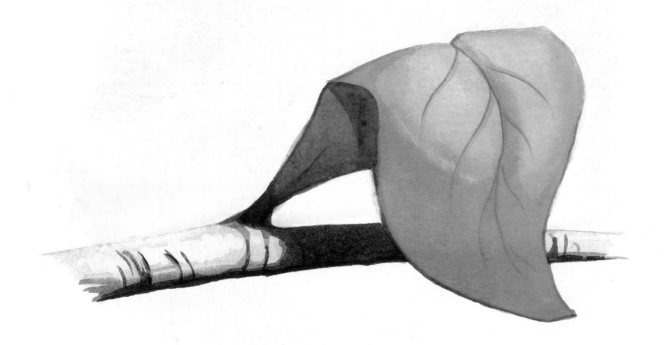

He said to himself, as the other leaves flew,
"If I want to stay here, that's just what I'll do."
"I have a good life where I'm living right now.
Why would I ever leave home, anyhow?"

A very old evergreen standing nearby
Was listening quietly, breathing a sigh.

She smiled at Luigi while he kept complaining
All through the night, even when it was raining.

Luigi soon turned to this weathered old pine
And said, "Do you really think I'm out of line"

"For wanting to stay here at home all the time?
Is being a homebody really a crime?"

"I'm safe and secure, standing here in your shade.
But you are an evergreen – you've got it made."

"You don't have leaves that get blown up and down
And maybe end up in a strange part of town."

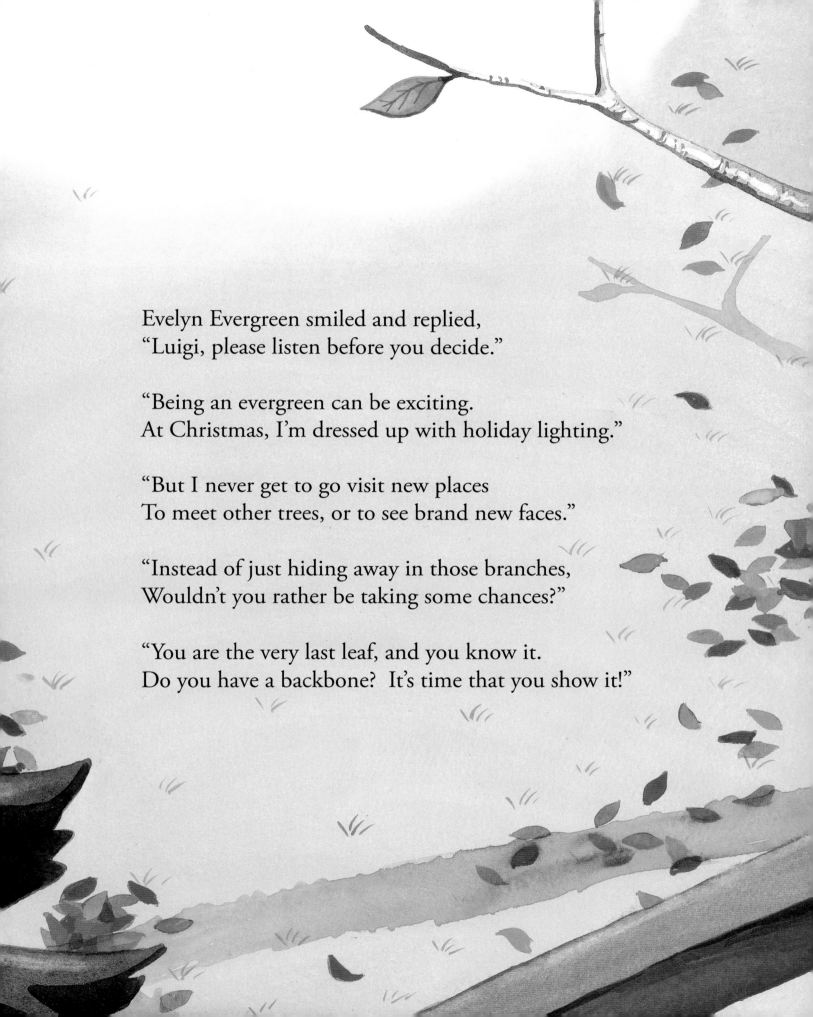

Evelyn Evergreen smiled and replied,
"Luigi, please listen before you decide."

"Being an evergreen can be exciting.
At Christmas, I'm dressed up with holiday lighting."

"But I never get to go visit new places
To meet other trees, or to see brand new faces."

"Instead of just hiding away in those branches,
Wouldn't you rather be taking some chances?"

"You are the very last leaf, and you know it.
Do you have a backbone? It's time that you show it!"

Though leaves don't have backbones, he knew what she meant.
It's true he was stubborn, but was he content?

He watched as the other leaves danced through the air,
And then he decided he'd finally dare

To try something new and leave fate to the wind.
He stood up as tall as he could, and he grinned.

Luigi was small, but he felt very big,

As a brisk autumn breeze pulled him right off his twig.

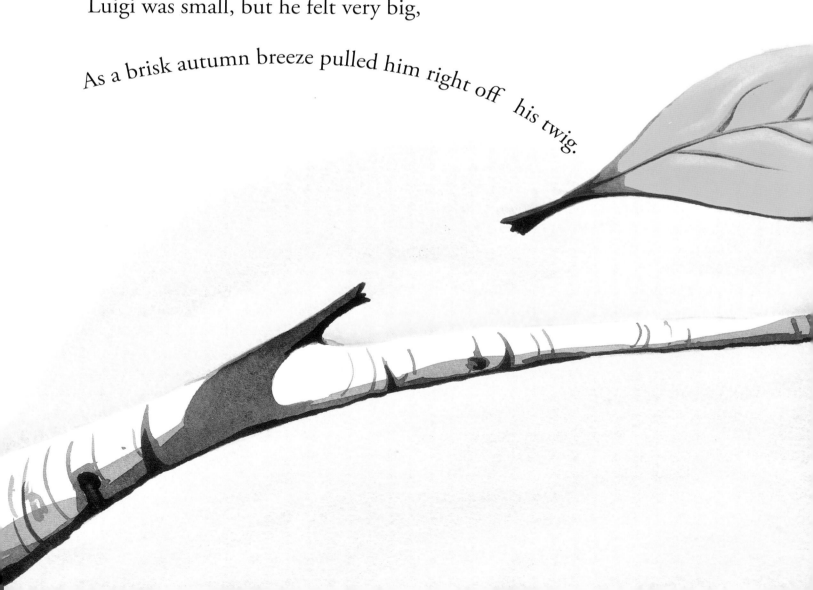

It blew and it blew as he flew through the sky.
He couldn't believe he could fly up so high.

He floated a while, then he soared past a cloud.
Luigi felt brave…he felt bold…he felt proud.

He loved being out and about on his own,
To travel the world and explore the unknown.

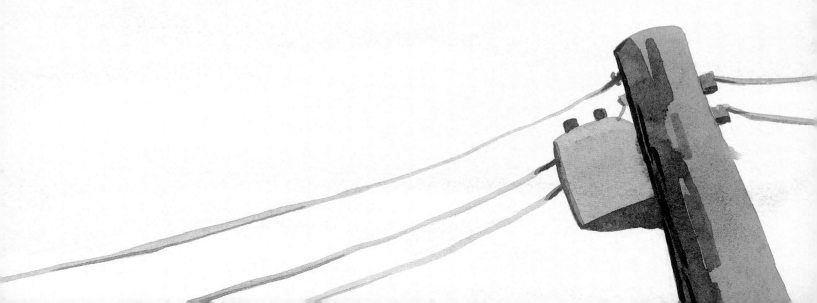

He sailed over lakes and he flew by a fountain.
He drifted along near the foot of a mountain.

He wondered where else he might go before dark,
As he cruised across town to the old city park.

He slid down the slide, all the way to the ground,
Then he raced for a ride on the merry-go-round.

A breeze came along and he started to flutter.
He flipped and he flopped and he fell in a gutter.

With oak leaves and elm leaves and maples and ash.
They all said hello, then decided to dash

Down to a yard where an old man was raking.
They hopped to the top of the pile he was making.

It was time for Luigi to take a short rest,
So another breeze lifted him up to a nest.

He saw baby birds being fed by their mother,
And tucked into bed, one right after the other.

He suddenly noticed the tree, tall and strong.
It's the evergreen tree that he'd known all along.

He circled the tree for a minute and then,
Evelyn smiled when she saw him again.

"How was your trip? I've been waiting to hear
If it was worth it, to face your old fear."

Luigi replied, "I have traveled quite far,
But tomorrow I plan to fly up to a star!"

"At first, I was yellow; today I'm bright red.
You were right all along – I had nothing to dread."

He fell fast asleep, as the old tree was beaming.
She cuddled him close while Luigi was dreaming.

Her tired old branches were filled with delight
As Evelyn Evergreen called it a night.

Then the sun left the sky, and the moon cast a glow
On a brave little leaf in a tree down below.

I am the girl who had planted the tree
Where Luigi once lived with my family and me.

And I am the one who has written this story,
But Evelyn really should get all the glory.

She told me in detail, beginning to end,
About the adventures of her little friend.

So where is he now? Is he up in the trees?

To look for Luigi, just follow the breeze.